To Aixa, who brings so much joy to our family, and special thanks to Asa and Dorian for your support and love.

- MeKael -

Dedicated to Dot, Paw Paw, and Grandpa Chuck

The FEARLESS PRINCESS

BY: MEKAEL C. BLACK

ILLUSTRATED BY : YENUSHKA DUNUWILA

Hi! I'm Aisha Sarai, but I love for my friends to call me Sarai. I wear a crown because Sarai means "my princess."

01

I'm going to tell you how this princess overcame all her fears!

When I wake up in the middle of the night,
and it's dark, I will not be in fright.

04

It's the first day of school. New teacher and new students-what will I do?

05

I will not be scared. I will be cool because God whispered in my ear, "I am with you."

06

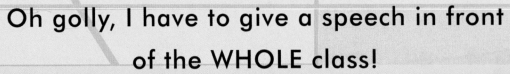

Oh golly, I have to give a speech in front of the WHOLE class!

No jitters here, because God did not give me a spirit of fear!

Oh no, it's a bug!

Do I run? Do I scream?

Wait! It's just a slug.

Slugs are squishy but not mean.

I'm so glad God was watching over me!

My parents bought me a new bike.

It's pretty, but it's tall!

I don't want to fall.

My brother told me not to think like that at all.

He said, "You can do it!" He was right! I can do it!
I will do it!

I'm doingggggggggggg it!

I can do all things through Christ who strengthens me.

A kid was really mean to me at school.
I told my teacher. I told my parents, and
we said a prayer, "Sarai is strong and courageous.
She will not be afraid of a mean kid, for the Lord
goes with Sarai!" My big brother also told me,
"You may be small physically, but you're big
spiritually!"

Guess what? The next day, the kid apologized to me. Now, we play together at recess.

The weatherman said a BIG storm was coming.

At first, I got scared.

BREAKING NEWS

24/7   Big Storm is Coming

My dad read a story where Jesus calmed
the storm. Jesus told the storm, "Peace! Be still,"
and it was still! I looked out the window, pointed
my hand to the sky, and shouted, "Peace! Be still!"
I felt so brave, and I was no longer afraid.

It was the day of my first piano recital. I was
supposed to be excited, but I was having nervous
thoughts. "What if I forget the notes?
What if the people laugh? What if I fall off my seat?"
I looked at my parents, and my parents smiled at me.
I could hear their voices saying, "God is with you,
Sarai. He gave you a gift to use for His glory.
He delights in you!"

I took a deep breath, adjusted my seat, played my song, and I got a standing ovation!

My parents enrolled me in swim lessons.
Why did they do that? I didn't ask for that!
I CAN'T swim!

19

My mom said, "God has given
you strength and courage! You will learn to be
a great, fearless swimmer." By the end of the
class, I was diving in the pool! Mom was right.
I did it!

I was sad and scared when I found out that I had to say goodbye to grandpa. My dad prayed with me, "Sarai, God's peace is with you; do not be worried and afraid. Grandpa is in Heaven, and we will see him again."

21

I felt so happy after we prayed. God is with me, and my memories of Grandpa are with me forever.

I'm so thankful that God is always with me. I have zero reasons to fear. When fear comes, I will remember the times when I prayed to God. He heard my prayers and answered me. He gave me His peace to overcome all my fears.

And, that's how I became the Fearless Princess!
I AM NOT AFRAID!
I am fearfully and wonderfully made.

PLEASE LEAVE A REVIEW

Please take a moment to rate and review
The Fearless Princess on Amazon as this helps
others (kids and parents) discover the story.
Authors love to hear from their readers!

Thank you and BE FEARLESS!

Made in the USA
Monee, IL
16 November 2022

17914666R00019